# The Mouse of Amherst

### by Elizabeth Spires
### Pictures by Claire A. Nivola

Frances Foster Books
Farrar, Straus and Giroux
New York

Library of Congress Cataloging-in-Publication Data
Spires, Elizabeth.
  The mouse of Amherst / Elizabeth Spires ; pictures by Claire  Nivola. — 1st ed.
    p.   cm.
  "Frances Foster Books."
  Summary: When she moves into Emily Dickinson's bedroom, Emmaline the
mouse discovers her own propensity for poetry.
  ISBN 0-374-35083-3
  [1. Mice--Fiction.  2. Dickinson, Emily, 1830-1886--Fiction.  3. Poetry--Fiction.]
I. Nivola, Claire A., ill.  II. Title.
PZ7.S7568Mo     1999
[Fic]—dc21                                                    98-17758

Poetry used by permission of the publishers and the Trustees of Amherst College from
*The Poems of Emily Dickinson*, Thomas H. Johnson, ed., Cambridge, Mass.: The Belknap
Press of Harvard University Press, Copyright © 1951, 1955, 1979, 1983 by the
President and Fellows of Harvard College.

Excerpts from letters 265, 342a, 342b (quoted on pages 32, 33, and 35) used by
permission of the publishers from *The Letters of Emily Dickinson*, edited by Thomas H.
Johnson, Cambridge, Mass.: The Belknap Press of Harvard University Press, Copyright
© 1958, 1986 by the President and Fellows of Harvard College.

*For my mother and Celia*

*⌒E. S.*

*By Chivalries as tiny,*
*A Blossom, or a Book,*
*The seeds of smiles are planted--*
*Which blossom in the dark.*

*⌒E.D.*

*For Nafu*
*How could a body so small*
*contain such a large heart?*

*⌒C. A. N.*

*I am a mouse*, a white mouse. My name is Emmaline. Before I met Emily, the great poet of Amherst, I was nothing more than a crumb gatherer, a cheese nibbler, a mouse-of-little-purpose. There was an emptiness in my life that nothing seemed to fill.

All that changed the day I moved into the Dickinson residence on Main Street. Preferring quiet quarters, I chose an upstairs bedroom as far away as possible from the clatter of the kitchen and the claws of the cat.

It was a light, airy room with four large windows, a single bed, a chest of drawers, a writing table and chair.

My room in the wainscoting was just as simple and pleasant, with a solitary bed and bureau, a quilt of colorful scraps, and a chair and table.

A quill pen and an inkwell sat on the table. The simple beauty of the pen, with its tall white arching feather, made me imagine a wing ready to take flight. Then I noticed, half-hidden under the inkwell, a note left by the previous tenant:

*Day by day and year by year,*
*You soon will find by living here*
*That words you thought you knew so well—*
*Big ones, small ones, short ones, tall ones—*
*Words in every shape and size*
*Hold many meanings, more surprise*
*Than you would give them credit for!*

I pondered the note, almost like a riddle, as I unpacked my valise. I always traveled lightly, with only a winter cape, a fleece robe and hot-water bottle for the brutal New England winters, and a small dictionary to help me improve my vocabulary.

I set my notebook, a gift from my parents when I first went out into the world, on the table. I seldom used it. I was not much of a letter writer, list maker, or note taker. I didn't keep a diary. Still, seeing it there next to the pen made me feel immediately at home.

At first the Dickinson residence struck me as an ordinary household. There was Mr. Dickinson, a silver-haired gentleman in a black suit who never smiled and was rarely there—

Mrs. Dickinson, a quiet nervous woman who kept out of Mr. Dickinson's way as much as possible and spent her days doing needlework and embroidery—

Lavinia, Emily's sister, who oversaw the house and was always busy in the kitchen cooking, baking, canning, and preserving—

and, of course, Emily, in her white dress. She always wore white. She seemed to be everywhere and nowhere at once, fluttering through the house like a ghost, stirring up a batch of gingerbread in the kitchen, or walking in the garden, lost in reverie. Like me, she was a nature lover and would often bring something in from the garden to study—a flower, a leaf, a mushroom, and, once, a dead bee!

It must have been Fate that steered me to choose Emily's bedroom for my own. My proximity gave me a chance to observe her closely. Whenever I heard her pattering footsteps coming up the stairs, I would retreat and wait for the hem of her white dress to brush past my doorway, stirring up a small cloud of dust. Peeking out, I would see her sit down at her desk, the look on her face one of utter concentration. Then she would pick up her pen and begin scribbling madly. *Scratch, scratch, scratch* went the pen for what seemed a small eternity. Usually after a half hour or so, Emily would put down the pen with a look of supreme satisfaction, as if she had just created a magnificent cheese soufflé.

At all times of the day and night, the same thing happened. What on earth was she writing? A diary? Letters? If so, why didn't she mail them? Instead, when she was finished, she always gathered up the loose sheets, stacked them neatly in a box, put the box in the drawer of her writing table, and shut the drawer firmly. This went on for several weeks and I despaired of ever solving the mystery of Emily Dickinson.

Not everyone in the Dickinson household took so warm an interest in Emily's scribbling as I did. The burdens of housekeeping seemed to fall most heavily upon Lavinia, and sometimes she was cross. One warm sunny day she interrupted Emily at her writing table, placed her hands upon her hips, and cried aloud:

"Sister, you are lost to the world. Why, a mouse might run across your hand while you are scrawling and you would take no notice of it."

Behind the wainscot, my whiskers pricked. It seemed certain that my presence was suspected. But Lavinia soon enough went off, and Emily was again bent over her desk, scribbling away, a small blizzard of paper around her. All the windows in the room were open, the filmy white curtains rising and falling in the gentle breeze. Suddenly an unexpected gust of wind blew sharply across the room, scattering half-sheets everywhere. A small scrap landed near my doorway. I made up my mind that I *had* to see what was written on it, even if I perished as a result of my curiosity.

I dashed out, snatched up the scrap, and ran back

into my room. Finally I would know what preoccupied Emily to such a great degree. For a minute I had trouble reading Emily's peculiar, slanting handwriting. Then the words fell into place, and I felt my face turn crimson, as if I were reading someone's private diary:

*If I can stop one Heart from breaking*
*I shall not live in vain*
*If I can ease one Life the Aching*
*Or cool one Pain*

*Or help one fainting Robin*
*Unto his Nest again*
*I shall not live in Vain.*

Imagine my surprise when I realized I was holding a poem! The words *spoke* to me. These were my feelings exactly, but ones I had always kept hidden for fear the world would think me a sentimental fool. I felt giddy and inspired, as if a whirligig were spinning in my brain. Almost without thinking, I sat down at my table, picked up my quill pen, and began writing on the back of Emily's poem. Words poured out of me in a torrent:

*I am a Little Thing.*
*I wear a Little Dress.*
*I go about my Days and Nights*
*Taking little barefoot Steps.*

*But though You never notice me*
*Nor count me as your Guest,*
*My Soul can soar as High as yours*
*And Hope burns in my chest!*

My hand trembled and my heart beat rapidly as I read what I had just written. Was it possible that *I* was a poet? I scarcely dared to believe it. And yet I had just written something that expressed my deepest feelings. From what secret place had my words come?

✦ ✦ ✦

That evening, while Emily was downstairs, I copied my poem into my notebook, making a few small improvements, and returned Emily's poem to her desk. Would she notice *my* poem on the back of hers? Would she be able to read my minuscule script? Then I fell into a restless sleep, dreaming jumbled lines from nursery rhymes and Shakespeare, all the poetry my mother had taught me as a child.

The next morning I was surprised to see a neatly folded sheet of paper wedged under my doorsill. There was no name or address on it, and yet I felt certain it was for me:

> *I'm Nobody! Who are you?*
> *Are you—Nobody—too?*
> *Then there's a pair of us!*
> *Don't tell! they'd banish us—you know!*
>
> *How dreary—to be—Somebody!*
> *How public—like a Frog—*
> *To tell your name—the livelong June—*
> *To an admiring Bog!*

Emily had read my poem and written back! I felt sure her poem was about the two of us, two "Nobodies" in a world that cared more about fame and

fortune than about words and feelings. Again, my heart
began to pound. Dizzy and flushed as the day before, I
sat down at my writing table and penned confidently:

> It matters what we think,
> What words we put in ink.
> It matters what we feel,
> What feelings we conceal.
>
> My pen is writing this,
> Words whirl in my brain.
> Is that what Poetry is?
> A pleasurable pain!

I put the pen down, surprised and delighted by my
words. I especially liked the part about "a pleasurable
pain," even though I wasn't quite sure what I meant by
that. Perhaps I *was* a poet! After making a copy for
myself, I again put the sheet with Emily's poem and
mine back on the blotter of her writing table.

I seemed to lose all sense of time when I was writing.

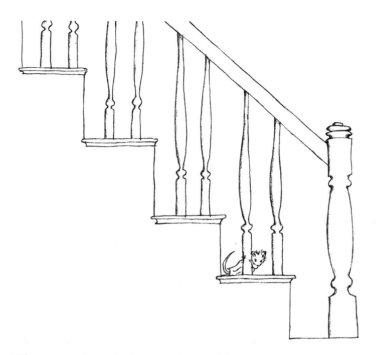

The morning had passed quickly, and I had missed breakfast. Ravenous—creatures of my kind usually are—I hoped the midday meal was near. When the clock struck one, I cautiously made my way down to the dining room. The Dickinsons, of course, always ate first, and I, the uninvited guest, contented myself with their crumbs and leavings. Today I hoped they would not tarry between courses.

Hidden from sight, I watched Lavinia carry in a delicious-looking cheese plate which she set out on the table. The intermingled smells of Cheddar, Swiss, and blue were sweet torture to my soul. As the courses were brought in, my famished brain made a perfect picture of the feast:

*Crumbs fell off the table,*
*Came crashing to the floor—*
*And I—a church mouse to the last—*
*Came scurrying for more.*

*Under the dining-room table*
*I hid my small self fast—*
*While shadows lunched in leisure—*
*Enjoying a fine repast.*

*A mountain of sugar glistened*
*In a snow-white sugar bowl—*
*A silver urn poured coffee—*
*And cream was a waterfall.*

*Voices spoke politely—*
*"Please pass me more of that"—*
*My heart stopped for a moment*
*When I thought I heard the Cat.*

*To eat too little is a shame—*
*To eat too much—a Sin—*
*I wait for the end of their dinner*
*So that my feast may begin.*

Hunger, or the intoxication of my verses, must have gotten the better of me. Lavinia's skirts were barely whisking from the room when I scampered onto the table before my time. She must have seen me, though I was insensible of her. A moment later, as I tiptoed toward the cheeseboard, the kitchen door reopened and Lavinia, with a meaningful look my way, thrust the cat into the room.

With a single savage bound the cat was on the table, advancing toward me. His eyes glowed green, his teeth were honed to needle points, pale foam hung from his lips. In my mad haste to avoid him, I overturned a cup. The coffee ran and stained the tablecloth.

I flung myself headlong on the floor, but still the cat was hot on my heels. I scrabbled frantically along the skirting board, but there was no hole, no crack, not the least retreat for me. The cat's breath was warm upon my back as I drew in a breath for my dying squeal—

It was the door hinge that cried instead. Emily was in the room, smacking the cat roundly with a rough twig broom, sending him yowling into the corner.

"Out, sir!" she cried, and swept him into the kitchen. As Lavinia put her inquiring head into the room, Emily gestured at the spilled cup, as if to blame the cat for what had happened—

"Look there, see what he's done..."

Emily must have sensed I was somewhere near. As she retreated from the room, she let a small scrap of paper flutter to the floor near my hiding place in the

cupboard. The sentiments on it were immediately sobering:

> *Papa above!*
> *Regard a Mouse*
> *O'erpowered by the Cat!*
> *Reserve within thy kingdom*
> *A "Mansion" for the Rat!*
>
> *Snug in seraphic Cupboards*
> *To nibble all the day,*
> *While unsuspecting Cycles*
> *Wheel solemnly away!*

How thoroughly Emily had entered into my soul to share my dread! In imagining the worst, she had also imagined a paradise . . . of sorts. Although I preferred not to consider the awful consequences of finding myself nose to nose with the cat, I was secretly pleased to find myself in one of her poems. We were fast becoming friends!

I left the dining room by a circuitous route, the better to avoid the cat, and took a turn in the garden with Emily. Together, we reveled in every flower, bird, and bee. I lounged in the shade of a mushroom, feeling both lazy and exhilarated. Emily picked a daffodil, breathed it in deeply, and dashed off the following:

> *Perhaps you'd like to buy a flower,*
> *But I could never sell—*
> *If you would like to* borrow,
> *Until the Daffodil*
>
> *Unties her yellow Bonnet*
> *Beneath the village door,*
> *Until the Bees, from Clover rows*
> *Their Hock, and Sherry, draw,*
>
> *Why, I will lend until just then,*
> *But not an hour more!*

Reading Emily's poem, I thought how unpredictable life could be. Who would have guessed that in the brief time I had been with the Dickinsons, I would have found my calling? That Emily and I would be sharing our poems with each other? Every sight and sound conjured a line of poetry in me. Out on Main Street, a horse lazily clip-clopped by, the beat of its hooves like the *ti-tum, ti-tum, ti-tum* of a poem. I recalled my restless dreams of the night before and determined to capture them:

> *Last night I rode a fiery Steed—*
> *It Galloped all night long.*
> *The Ringing of its Hoofbeats*
> *Was like a Drummer's Song.*
>
> *I wonder as I ride my Horse*
> *If it is riding Me.*
> *And when I wonder such a thing*
> *I know it's Poetry!*

✤ ✤ ✤

It was soon after our idyll in the garden that Emily had a visitor. I might have missed the episode entirely had I not been in the front parlor at the time, thoroughly engrossed in removing the stuffing from one of the Dickinsons' armchairs. It is a habit that my kind are prone to, though *why* I cannot explain.

There was a firm knock at the front door. A moment later, a Mr. Higginson, in whiskers and waistcoat, was shown into the parlor by the maid. He scanned the room importantly, then moved with purpose toward me, lowering himself heavily into the very chair where I was concealed! Wedged between cushion and chair back, I could scarcely move or breathe.

Then Emily entered. She held a bouquet of daylilies in her outstretched hand and said, in a soft breathless whisper—

"These are my introduction—forgive me if I am frightened—I never see strangers—and hardly know what to say—"

The daylilies were set in a vase on the mantel. Higginson attempted small talk. Actually, Emily did most of the talking, as if she had saved up a year's worth of conversation to spend in one afternoon.

"If I read a book," she told him, "and it makes my whole body so cold no fire ever can warm me, I know *that* is poetry. If I feel physically as if the top of my head were taken off, I know *that* is poetry. These are the only way I know it. Is there any other way?"

Higginson was silent, as if a strange creature had just posed him a riddle. He coughed politely into his handkerchief and shifted his weight. I took that moment to free myself and scamper over the back of the chair. Then I scrabbled up to the mantel and hid behind the vase, the better to see and hear.

The talk came around to Emily's own poems, which, I gathered, she had sent to Higginson's magazine. For no reason I could explain, I felt a sinking feeling in the pit of my stomach.

"Miss Dickinson," he began reluctantly, his face clouding over, "your verses are *alive* but . . . spasmodic. Uncontrolled —"

*Uncontrolled!* My blood boiled at the word.

"I suggest"—at this point he faltered—"that you delay to publish."

Outraged at Higginson's opinion, and without stop-
ping to consider the consequences of my actions, I gave
the vase a mighty heave. It teetered on the mantel's
edge, then crashed to the floor, missing him by a hair.

Higginson leaped up, terrified. His eyes swung wildly around the room but could find no cause for the bombardment. Hidden behind the mantel clock, I savored my small revenge.

Emily pretended to ignore the mishap entirely. She gave Higginson an enigmatic smile and answered him coolly—

"Mr. Higginson—if Fame belonged to me, I could not escape her—if she did not, the longest day would pass on the chase—my Barefoot Rank is better—"

Rather too quickly, I thought, Higginson made his excuses to go, saying that he would come again, "*Sometime*."

To that Emily replied, "Say in a long time. That will be nearer."

Higginson left. Emily vanished upstairs. I gathered the daylilies, scattered on the carpet, but it was no use. They were wilted completely.

To my great relief, Higginson's visit seemed only to spur Emily on. We fell into a routine. At any hour, wherever inspiration found her, Emily would jot down her thoughts—on scraps of paper, on the backs of old envelopes, on wrappers and labels—and leave them on

my doorstep. And I, willing correspondent, would reply. We wrote about nature and the seasons, we exchanged letters, we even tried our hand at riddles.

Several happy weeks ensued. And then one day, a

letter arrived for Emily which she did not open but, instead, clasped to her breast in noticeable agitation. From an admirer? Or perhaps a rejection from another thick-headed editor who did not understand her rhymes?

At supper, she said not a word, but sat distracted and withdrawn. Lavinia attempted to converse, but Emily would have no part.

"Sister, have you seen a ghost?" Vinnie gently questioned. "Tonight you are as pale as one."

With that, just as a lovely cheesecake was being served, Emily fled to her room weeping. Neither Lavinia nor Mr. and Mrs. Dickinson, more accustomed to Emily's moods than I, tried to stop her.

Long past midnight, the floorboards creaking, Emily paced back and forth, back and forth. Her chestnut hair, unpinned, streamed wildly around her shoulders. She began a poem, then crumpled the sheet with an anguished cry. Her sleeve knocked against the ink bottle, spilling a rough blot of ink on her white nightgown. She took no notice.

As if buffeted by violent winds, she rose again to pace. In mute agony, again she sat down at her desk. Finally, with a despairing sigh, she took out another clean sheet. The white paper crackled with electricity as she smoothed it on her blotter. Words tumbled out of her pen like lightning etching the sky on a stormy night:

*Wild Nights—Wild Nights!*
*Were I with thee*
*Wild Nights should be*
*Our luxury!*

*Futile—the Winds—*
*To a Heart in port—*
*Done with the Compass—*
*Done with the Chart!*

*Rowing in Eden—*
*Ah, the Sea!*
*Might I but moor—Tonight—*
*In Thee!*

Dear Emily! She stood alone in a place I could not touch. Or could I? How could I convince her that even the darkest night had a dawn? Outside, in the east, I was surprised to see a faint light—a ray of hope! Inspired, I wrote:

> *I stepped out on the Lawn*
> *To watch another Dawn—*
> *"Her Majesty" would soon arrive,*
> *And Darkest Night be gone.*

*The Sun stepped over the horizon—*
*Her dress was orange and red.*
*I made a curtsy to "Her Grace"*
*And then I bowed my head.*

*Slowly, She began to rise*
*And nodded I could, too.*
*Amazed, I saw around me*
*The tattered World made new!*

Finished, I looked up. Emily was fast asleep, her head pillowed on the hard wood of her writing table as if it were the softest down. On tiptoe, I crept past her and gently snuffed out the candle.

My poem must have been a comfort to her. The next morning was considerably calmer. Emily rose, pinned up her hair, and put on a clean white smock. Outside her window, a little bird sang a lighthearted song, as if the night had never happened. Calmly, Emily took up her pen and composed:

*"Hope" is the thing with feathers—*
*That perches in the soul—*
*And sings the tune without the words—*
*And never stops—at all—*

*And sweetest—in the Gale—is heard—*
*And sore must be the storm—*
*That could abash the little Bird*
*That kept so many warm—*

*I've heard it in the chillest land—*
*And on the strangest Sea—*
*Yet, never, in Extremity,*
*It asked a crumb—of Me.*

Then she went down to the kitchen to bake a pan of gingerbread. Emily's gingerbread was famous in Amherst, especially among the children. Often, hidden from sight, she lowered them sweet tidbits in a picnic basket from her bedroom window. It was a game to her, and one the children loved.

The heavenly smell of gingerbread slowly wafted up

the stairs, making my whiskers twitch. Prudently I decided not to venture down to the kitchen. The thought of a chance encounter with the cat sent a chill down my spine. On the windowsill, the picnic basket sat in an inviting patch of sunlight. I climbed in, pulled a gingham napkin over my head, and settled down for a short, sweet nap.

I must have fallen into a deep sleep. Suddenly I awoke, violently tossed about. The picnic basket tipped and swung on a long rope in the open air. I peeked over the edge and saw, with shock and horror, the hands of a dozen screaming children reaching up, outstretched. Each wanted to be the first to snatch a square of Emily's gingerbread. A hideous, involuntary *squeak!* came from my lips. Escape was paramount, but my tail was caught in the basket's woven strands. Desperately I worked it free. Then I summoned all my agility and clambered up the thin string like a common rat on a ship's rigging.

At the sill, I closed my eyes and jumped. I landed with a small thud on the hooked rug, skidded wildly across the floor, and took a pratfall. A comedy . . . to everyone but me.

Then I ran, ran, on all fours to my mouse hole. In the safety of my room, I righted myself and tried in vain to dust off my petticoats. Hot tears streamed down my face. How ashamed I was! In a desperate moment I had thought not of my dignity as mouse and poet but only of my own wretched salvation. Furious at my pounding heart, I wrote:

> *Heart, Heart, why do you beat like that?*
> *Is it because you thought you heard the Cat?*
> *Is it because the Owl sharpens its claws?*
>
> *O Heart, why such a racket?*
> *What are the facts? What is the cause?*
> *And the Heart replies, how quietly it replies,*
>
> *"It is because it's fearful being Small."*

I believe Emily was sorry for the embarrassment she had caused me. When I recovered myself a little, I saw she had left a thimbleful of elderberry wine and a crumb of gingerbread outside my door.

And then occurred a most frightful episode, which I still shudder to recall. I might have seen it coming. There were warning signs: the way Lavinia cocked her head to listen, or ran her fingers down the skirting boards of Emily's room on those rare occasions when her sister let her in to clean. I should not have been surprised when, at supper one night, Lavinia broke out:

"Emily! This has gone on long enough! There are mice in your room, yes, mice, and even worse, perhaps! Crumbs, dust, disorder—there's no wonder! But tomorrow, we must have the *ratcatcher*!"

I ought to have left that very night, but somehow could not draw myself away. Was it some dreadful fascination, as when a mouse stands mesmerized before the scaly eye of an approaching snake? No, I think some kinder impulse held me fast. Emily was long at her table that night, writing by the light of her stuttering candle. Devotedly I watched, and at last fell asleep, my nose laid across the threshold of my doorsill . . .

Morning brought a rude awakening: Lavinia's shrill "Emily! He's come! The ratcatcher's come! Come out and let him do his work!"

Emily was up and dressed already, or perhaps she had not slept at all. She argued with them through the door. She did not wish to be disturbed, she would not let them in at all, or if she must, she would not leave. At length there was a little pause, and Emily turned toward the room. Was it the air itself that she addressed, or me?

"I will not have them ferret me out," she declared. "Nor you."

Then, reaching into her apron pocket, she moved toward my mouse hole. By old habit, I withdrew into the shadows, but I saw what she took out, and I was dumbstruck. It was a *mousetrap*—springloaded, with a cruel wire to break my back. Was it possible my Emily

would betray me so? Unbelieving, I watched her thrust
it through my door.

I backed away, but kept my vantage. I could still see
the door to Emily's room. The whiskered ratcatcher
came in in his baggy trousers, Lavinia avidly peering
over his shoulder. He held a cloth sack in his hand in
which something sinuously moved. As he unloosed the

drawstring, a chilly terror froze my bones—

A stoat, white-furred, red-eyed, and ready to work his way through any crack or cranny—there'd be no hole where I might hide from him. No sooner had his claws struck the floorboards than he flew toward my door like an arrow from a bow. I could not move—and

did not need to, for instantly the mousetrap snapped shut across his nose.

The stoat rolled into a ball with a horrible shriek, thrashing the trap against the table leg, while the rat-catcher cursed and tried to get him free. Emily sought to hide her titter behind her fingers, while Lavinia fumed and glowered. But there was nothing Lavinia could do . . . for the moment.

✢ ✢ ✢

For the moment only. I wondered what would be next from Lavinia. Poison? Or perhaps a terrier pulling up the floorboards? For I was sure Lavinia would not relent. I saw I must decide once and for all whether to leave the Dickinsons'—as Emily never would. For although she was content with her life's "circumference," narrow but infinitely deep, I felt stirred to see more of life.

I weighed my choices. To go? To venture into the wide world, to take my chances, to have my adventures? To write my epic? But also, to expose myself, a sheltered mouse, to perils beyond my imagination.

Or—to stay? To spend years in deepening friendship with Emily, happily exchanging poems. And yet to chafe at my second-rate status in the house. To live my days tiptoeing around the cat.

As if she could read my thoughts, Emily chose that

very moment to leave me a poem. Did she know her words had the power to change the course of my life?

> *On this wondrous sea*
> *Sailing silently,*
> *Ho! Pilot, ho!*
> *Knowest thou the shore*
> *Where no breakers roar—*
> *Where the storm is o'er?*
>
> *In the peaceful west*
> *Many the sail at rest—*
> *The anchors fast—*
> *Thither I pilot thee—*
> *Land Ho! Eternity!*
> *Ashore at last!*

Emily's poem made me feel the vastness of the universe, and a lonely sailor's desire for both adventure and safe harbor. I recalled a night from my childhood, my parents fast asleep in the nest, when I had ventured outside alone for the first time. As I lay on my back in the black grass, gazing up at the white-hot moon and stars, powerful emotions had washed over me—joy and wonder at being alive, fear for my own safety, and a longing to touch something untouchable. Who was I? Why I was here? Where was I going?

My half-packed valise sat waiting. Putting it aside, I labored to recapture the memory. My feather pen, hot and bright once more, moved quickly over the page:

*I sailed on a Leaf*
*By the name of Belief*
*Over the wide, wide Sea—*

*The Moon on my left—*
*The Stars on my right—*
*Were there to guide only me.*

*Alone and Free*
*It felt good to be Me*
*On the Ship of my Life—*BELIEF!

I left my poem behind as a parting gift. I'm quite sure Emily understood.

✣ ✣ ✣

I have made a keepsake of our friendship, a little book I have sewn together of Emily's poems. And mine. Immodestly, I've titled it *Emily and Emmaline: The Poems of Two Poets.*

I hardly know what my book's fate will be, or if other eyes will ever see it. But whatever happens, I shall remain philosophical, as I know Emily would. I began as a "Nobody" and I shall, most likely, end as a "Nobody." But along the way I have come to discover how infinitely mysterious words really are. I shall carry my book with me wherever I go, for I intend to keep writing.

Since that sad day when I took leave of Emily, my life has taken a surprising turn. It appears that I will not be the last of my kind to take pen to paper. You see, I now have a family. Among my children, I am proud to say, are more than a few writers who keep me busy with their scribbling and cross outs. Perhaps, a few years hence, one of them will search out my room at the Dickinsons' and meet Emily herself. I hope so. Until then, I remind them—

*There is no Frigate like a Book*
*To take us Lands away*
*Nor any Coursers like a Page*
*Of prancing Poetry—*
*This Travel may the poorest take*
*Without oppress of Toll—*
*How frugal is the Chariot* MOUSE'S
*That bears the ~~Human~~ soul.*

# About Emily Dickinson

❦

Emily Dickinson was born in Amherst, Massachusetts, on December 10th, 1830, in a large brick house on Main Street called the Homestead. Except for the year she attended Mount Holyoke Female Seminary (now Mount Holyoke College) when she was seventeen, she lived in her parents' house for her entire life. Neither Emily nor her sister Lavinia ever married. (Their brother, Austin, lived next door with his wife in a house called the Evergreens.)

No one knows exactly why, but over the years Emily gradually became a recluse. She strayed no farther than her own garden and rarely saw visitors. But although Emily withdrew from the life of Amherst, the townspeople knew who she was. In admiration, and perhaps puzzlement, they referred to her as "the Myth." Emily kept in touch with her friends far and near by writing letters, sometimes enclosing an enigmatic poem, riddle, or recipe. One of her poems, only two lines long, declares, "*A Letter is a joy of Earth —/It is denied the gods —* "

Emily wrote 1,789 poems during her lifetime, but published only a handful. Editors objected to her unusual rhymes and punctuation, and were disturbed by her odd, original way of seeing and saying things. The visit with "Mr. Higginson" (Thomas Wentworth Higginson), the editor of *The Atlantic Monthly*, really happened. Higginson, like many others, did not recognize her poetic genius and discouraged her from trying to publish her poems. Emily may have been disappointed, but she also held dear the quiet life she led as a "Nobody." One tiny poem expresses her divided feelings about "Fame":

> *Fame is a bee.*
> *It has a song—*
> *It has a sting—*
> *Ah, too, it has a wing.*

In 1886, when Emily was only fifty-five years old, she died of Bright's disease. Lavinia had known that Emily wrote poems, but she had no idea that Emily had written so many until she went through her sister's things after her death. Emily had secretly made about nine hundred of her poems into forty little hand-sewn packets, held together with twine; other poems had been scribbled down and saved on old wrappers, the backs of envelopes, and in the margins of newspapers.

Lavinia was determined to publish Emily's poems. With the help of a family friend, Mabel Loomis Todd, who deciphered Emily's almost illegible handwriting, the first edition of Emily's poems was published in 1890, four years after her death. "Poems" was an immediate success, and many more editions followed.

✢ ✢ ✢

Today Emily Dickinson is considered one of the most important poets who ever lived. Her house in Amherst is a national landmark open to the public. A visitor can stand in the upstairs bedroom, where she wrote many of her poems, see her white dress, or imagine Emily baking gingerbread in the kitchen or lost in reverie in the garden.

Perhaps because she lived an anonymous, outwardly uneventful life, Emily Dickinson felt a kinship with all things humble and small. One of her poems begins, "Grief is a mouse —/And chooses Wainscot in the Breast/For His Shy House —/And baffles quest…" And there is another poem of Emily's to consider. Did Emily actually write it? Or could it have been penned by her small friend Emmaline? Here is the poem:

*I was the slightest in the House —*
*I took the smallest Room —*
*At night, my little Lamp, and Book —*
*And one Geranium —*

*So stationed I could catch the Mint*
*That never ceased to fall —*
*And just my Basket —*
*Let me think — I'm sure*
*That this was all —*

*I never spoke — unless addressed —*
*And then, 'twas brief and low —*
*I could not bear to live — aloud —*
*The Racket shamed me so —*

*And if it had not been so far —*
*And any one I knew*
*Were going — I had often thought*
*How noteless — I could die —*

What do you think?